Become a star reader with Caillou!

This three-level reading series is designed for pre-readers or beginning readers and is based on popular Caillou episodes. The books feature common sight words used with limited grammar. Each book also offers a set number of target words. These words are noted in bold print and are presented in a picture dictionary in order to reinforce meaning and expand reading vocabulary.

Level 1
Little Star

For pre-readers to read along
- 125-175 words
- Simple sentences
- Simple vocabulary and common sight words
- Picture dictionary teaching 6 target words

Level 2
Rising Star

For beginning readers to read with support
- 175-250 words
- Longer sentences
- Limited vocabulary and more sight words
- Picture dictionary teaching 8 target words

Level 3
Super Star

For improving readers to read on their own or with support
- 250-350 words
- Longer sentences and more complex grammar
- Varied vocabulary and less-common sight words
- Picture dictionary teaching 10 target words

Text: adaptation by Anne Paradis
Series Consultant: Rebecca Klevberg Moeller, Language Teaching Expert
All rights reserved.
Original story written by Marion Johnson, based on the animated series CAILLOU
Illustrations: Eric Sévigny, based on the animated series CAILLOU

The PBS KIDS logo is a registered mark of PBS and is used with permission.

Chouette Publishing would like to thank the Government of Canada and SODEC
for their financial support.

Books
Tax Credit

Gestion
SODEC

Bibliothèque et Archives nationales du Québec and Library and Archives
Canada cataloguing in publication

Paradis, Anne, 1972-
Caillou: the carrot patch
New edition.

(Read with Caillou. Level 2)
Previously published as: In the garden/Marion Johnson.

For children aged 3 and up.

ISBN 978-2-89718-367-7

1. Caillou (Fictitious character) - Juvenile fiction. 2. Gardening - Juvenile
fiction. 3. Carrots - Juvenile fiction. 4. Grandparent and child - Juvenile fiction.
I. Sévigny, Éric. II. Johnson, Marion, 1949-   . In the garden. III. Title. IV.
Title: Carrot patch.

PS8631.A713C34 2017   jC813'.6   C2016-941540-6
PS9631.A713C34 2017

Printed in China
10 9 8 7 6 5 4 3 2 1   CHO1955 FEB2017

The Carrot Patch

Text: Anne Paradis
Series Consultant: Rebecca Klevberg Moeller, Language Teaching Expert
Illustrations: Eric Sévigny, based on the animated series

Grandpa is making a **vegetable patch**.

Caillou is helping grandpa.

"Would you like to have your own garden, Caillou?"

"Yes, I would."

"Which **vegetable** would you like to grow?" Grandpa asks.

"I want to grow **carrots**!"
Caillou says.

Grandpa gives **carrot seeds** to Caillou.

Caillou sows the **seeds**.
Caillou waters the **seeds**.

"The **carrots** are not growing!"
Caillou says.

"**Carrots** grow slowly," Grandpa says.

Caillou makes a **marker**.

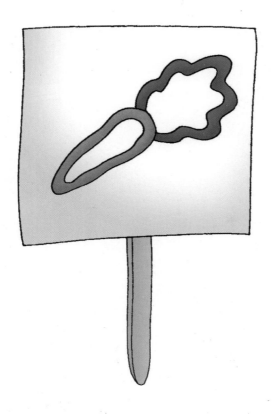

Caillou will know where the **carrots** are.

Every day Caillou checks his
carrot patch.

Every day Caillou waters his garden.

One day, Caillou sees green **leaves**.

The **carrots** are growing!

Every day Caillou checks the green **leaves**.

They are growing slowly.

Caillou sees a **squirrel**.

Caillou scares away the **squirrel**.

One day, the **carrots** are big
enough.

Caillou pulls on the **leaves**.
A **carrot** comes out of the **ground**.

Caillou and Grandpa pick the **carrots**.

Mommy cooks the **carrots**.

Caillou is proud.

Caillou tastes the **carrots**.

"Well done!" Mommy says.
"Yum!" Rosie says.

Picture Dictionary

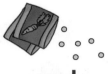

seeds

carrot

squirrel

leaves

marker

vegetable

patch

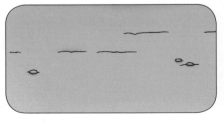

ground

"These are the best **carrots** ever!"